COZY CHRISTMAS CRUSH

A Mercy Mountain Holiday Novella

Copyright © 2021 by Becca Maxton

All rights reserved. Except for use in any review, the reproduction or utilization of this work in whole or in part in any form by any electronic, mechanical or other means, now known or hereinafter invented, including xerography, photocopying and recording, or in any information storage or retrieval system, is forbidden without the written permission of the publisher.

This is a work of fiction. Names, characters, places and incidents are either the product of the author's imagination or are used fictitiously, and any resemblance to actual persons, living or dead, business establishments, events or locales is entirely coincidental.

Printed in the USA.

Cover Design and Interior Format
© THE KILLION GROUP INC

COZY CHRISTMAS *Crush*

A
MERCY MOUNTAIN
Holiday
NOVELLA

Becca Maxton

Dedication

For Dad

*You can't catch a fish,
without a line in the water.*

Chapter 1

RAFE MOONEY PULLED HIS TRUCK into the gas station and cut the engine. This was the last gas station for fifty miles between Ashnee Valley, Colorado, and…well…anywhere else. At the pump ahead of him sat a mustard-colored Jeep SUV with temporary plates. A tall, slender woman with black pants, boots, and a short, white, puffy coat opened her gas tank cover. A fur-lined hood hid her face from view. He liked her red scarf and gloves. A classy flash of color.

Good snow tires on the vehicle, he noted. Any direction right now meant heading into a winter storm. The snow wasn't bad in the valley yet, but west of here had close to fifteen inches already, and according to weather warnings, the total was expected to accumulate to twenty-four inches or higher in the next two days.

Fortunately, he planned to head south to New Mexico to see his mom and dad for Christmas. At eighty years old, his parents didn't travel much anymore. He looked forward to a quiet holiday enjoying Mom's cooking, football on TV, and the short stack of books he'd been meaning to get to.

He set the gas pump to fill and went inside the small convenience store to grab a coffee for the road. When he returned, he gave a friendly wave to the lady in front of him, who waved back.

"Hi Rafe," she said and pushed her hood back. "It's me under here."

"Hey," Rafe said to Cindy Wheeler. Doc Cindy as everybody called her in town. Ashnee Valley's resident psychiatrist.

"I couldn't see your pretty. Your face. Meeting you here is…" He cringed. He always turned into a blithering idiot whenever she was near. "Fancy meeting you here."

Cindy walked his direction. "Are you heading home for Christmas?"

"I am. Is this a new SUV? You're keeping on top of the storm?"

"Brand new and yes I'm trying to keep ahead of the storm. I need to get a move-on though. I'm headed up to the mountains. It's coming in fast."

"Where are you going?" He asked.

"Hawkeye. I've rented a cabin for a week and a half, possibly two, depending on how long it takes me to finish the final revisions of my book."

"So, you're spending Christmas working. Why doesn't that surprise me." Rafe laughed.

Cindy tipped her head side-to-side. "I have a few fun things planned too. I'll have a tree to decorate. Plus, a couple new recipes to try." She shrugged. "How about you?"

Rafe closed his gas tank cover. "Seeing my folks. It will be nice." He grinned. "A break from working and all the Mannis family madness."

"They are a big, busy family, aren't they?" Cindy smiled.

"Especially with their Mercy Mountain Lodge having guests for the first time."

The wind had picked up in the short time they chatted. Ice chunks stuck to the fur on Cindy's hood.

"It's snowing," he said.

Okay blockhead, that's obvious.

"You're right. I better get going or I'll have to scrape the windows again. It's going to be late by the time I get up there."

Rafe glanced again at her SUV. It appeared loaded to the ceiling. "You have a lot of stuff in there."

"I do," she agreed. "A couple suitcases, tree decorations, my baking supplies, four coolers of food. Plus, my laptop and reference books, of course. I'm staying at that cabin until my work is done, come hell or high snow."

"How about I follow you up there to help you unload? I'm not in any hurry. I can get on the road a little later than planned tonight. My folks aren't expecting me any particular day or time as long as I arrive by Christmas."

Cindy put her red-gloved hand on his arm. "Thanks, Rafe. But that won't be necessary. I know how to drive in the snow. I've been up to Hawkeye before. I know the way."

"Yeah, but this is a big storm." He hesitated not

wanting to press too hard. "There's no cell reception for part of the way, until you're out of the canyon."

"That's true."

He took a glance at the sky. "It's dark already."

Cindy tilted her head, studying him. "You know what, I'm going to say yes. I guess I would feel more comfortable. It's a very generous offer. Thank you."

He flashed a lopsided grin. "I'm a guy." He shook his head. "I mean I'm a very generous guy."

"And you're sure," she asked without acknowledging his blunder, "it won't set you back too much on your trip?"

"Not at all. I'll follow, help you unpack and be on my way."

"Okay then, let's go." Cindy patted his arm.

He stood enthralled as she walked away, unable to avoid checking out her cute little butt in those pants. He'd been crushing on this woman since he saw her photo on the jacket of her first book years ago. Smart as a whip too. He'd read her book on sibling grief from cover to cover even though he had no personal experience with the topic as an only child.

Her SUV moved forward with two beeps to her horn, at which point he realized he still stood outside his truck daydreaming about her intelligence and those mesmerizing eyes the color of brandy. He got in the vehicle, set his coffee in the cup holder, started the engine, and pulled out of the gas station. At the light she waved at him in her review mirror. He blinked his headlights in response.

After an hour on the road, he had the windshield wipers going full speed as they wound their way through Dark Horse Canyon. Normally, he'd calculate they had another thirty minutes to go, but it might take longer once they got closer to Hawkeye and off the main road.

The cabins were familiar to him. He'd stayed there before with the Mannis brothers for fishing weekends. The last two miles had an especially steep pitch and the area overall remained isolated. Enormous relief had swept over him when Cindy agreed to his suggestion. She was independent and capable. He knew all that. Nonetheless, the thought of her vehicle possibly getting stuck in the snow made him shift uncomfortably in his seat, even now.

Cindy started pumping her brakes as they came toward the stop sign for the turn heading out of the canyon. Rafe chuckled at the adorable way she bounced in her seat, bopping her head back and forth in the SUV. She waved back at him again, then turned right. As he followed, he flipped on his radio and found a station playing "Jingle Bell Rock" imagining this to be the song she listened to.

He thought about the topic of her latest book. *The physical and emotional progression of intimacy in relationships.* She'd mentioned it back in September when he'd been at lunch with his friend Jim. He might be in his forties, but there could be something there to learn.

Maybe I'll invite her to lunch again after the book

comes out...to... discuss it more.

At the next turn, this time to the left, he followed her, heading up the incline to the cabins, keeping an eye on her SUV. His truck fish-tailed behind but he held his speed steady to reach the top of the hill. They were at eight thousand feet elevation with a nasty wind howling as he parked alongside her in front of one of the cabins.

Wasting no time, she had her hood back on and had opened her trunk by the time he got out of his truck. Cindy dragged two suitcases behind her through the snow on the short path to the front door. He came around to the back of her vehicle, put a box of books on top of one of the coolers and followed.

"You go inside," he said when they reached the door. "I'll bring the rest."

"You sure?"

He pulled his hat lower and nodded. "You'll probably need to get the heat turned up."

"I bet you're right." She found the key under the mat, unlocked the door, and stepped inside.

Rafe returned to the SUV, retrieving two plastic tubs labeled X-mas tree decorations. As he walked up the path again, the front porch light came on, guiding his return in the near white-out conditions. He'd need to take it slow going back through canyon before he could get on the highway to head south. Setting the tubs just inside the door, he made his way back and forth three more times to the Jeep.

"Thank you so much." Cindy walked toward him when he stepped inside and shut the cabin door. She was still wearing her coat but had removed her boots and turned on every light inside.

He surveyed the cozy living room with leather furniture and a big screen TV. The far wall had a huge window. It was too dark to tell what the view would be, whether forest or maybe she'd even be able to see down to the Talking Fish river.

"This is nicer than the cabins I've stayed in before."

"I didn't realize you'd been here," Cindy said as she picked up one of the coolers and set it on the small dining table-for-two next to the kitchen.

"I'm an honorary invitee to the Mannis fishing weekends." He smirked. "Now I can see they've been renting the cheap cabins."

Cindy laughed. "I'm not very rustic, as you can probably imagine. This is one of the fancy cabins. Would you like to come in to warm up for a bit?"

He glanced out the window closest to the front door at how the snow wasn't letting up. "I better not. It might take a while going back through the canyon." He put his hat back on his head. "Slow. I'll take it."

Nice speaking.

She walked his direction unzipping her coat and hung it, along with her scarf, on the hooks by the door.

"I think you should stay tonight. It's late and the snow isn't slowing down. There's a comfy couch, or so it looks. You could head out in the morning."

He shook his head. "No, thank you though. I'm going to hit the road. Good luck with your book. Merry Christmas."

She put her hands on her hips. "Did you feel relieved when I said yes to letting you follow me here?"

"What? Of course."

"Well, I'll feel the same sense of relief if you get some sleep and then leave for New Mexico when it's daylight."

He pushed his hat up, then pulled it down again.

"I'm going to worry," she added with a pointed look.

A smile tugged at the corner of his mouth. "You'd worry about me?"

She cocked an eyebrow. "I might even get angry if you go. I don't like to worry."

His grin broadened. "You're a psychiatrist who listens to people's darkest secrets and that doesn't make you worry?"

Her eyes glinted with humor.

"I have more control over that type of situation. I haven't figured out how to control weather. Come on." With a hand to his elbow, she turned him to the door. "Go get your stuff."

He hesitated on the porch as she held the door open about two inches to keep snow from coming inside. "There's a game on TV and one of the coolers is mostly beer," she shouted over the wind and shut the door.

Well, if you insist.

Chapter 2

IN THE FEW MINUTES IT took Rafe to get his bag from his truck, Cindy found extra blankets and a pillow and put them on a chair in the living room. She'd wheeled her suitcases into her bedroom. Now in the kitchen nook, she began unloading items from her coolers into the refrigerator.

"Here, let me take that bag." She walked toward him when he came back inside.

Besides his duffel bag, he carried a paper sack in the crook of his arm.

She put her hands out for the grocery bag. "Would you like to give that to me?" she said when he didn't move.

"Oh, yeah." He held the bag out. "Here. My contribution to the snacks."

She set the bag on the table and peeked in. "May I?"

"Sure."

She lifted a bottle of bourbon and set it on the table. Next two bags of pork rinds and finally a can of whipped cream. She tilted her head in Rafe's direction with a questioning look.

"Oh that. There's a story that goes with the whipped cream."

"I bet."

His booming laugh filled the tiny dining nook. "Not like that." He took off his coat and hung it next to hers on the hooks by the door.

"My mom is a fantastic cook and even better baker, but...she somehow never remembers the whipped cream for her desserts." He chuckled. "It's now sort of a family joke, I guess. I always bring a can when I visit."

"I love that story. I'll put it in the fridge and..." she glanced around the room and headed toward a particular cardboard box, "...write a note so you don't forget it in the morning."

She pulled a lime green pad of sticky-notes and a pen from the box, wrote a reminder, then stuck in on the front door. "There."

"You're a very organized woman."

"That's no secret. You know what is?" she asked as she walked back to the kitchen and continued unpacking. "Unlike your mother, I am a mediocre cook and horrifyingly bad at baking."

Rafe set his boots on the mat near the door and glanced up.

She laughed. "You should see your expression. I believe forlorn is the word."

He carried his duffel bag to the corner of the living room and walked back.

"I'm surprised," he said with a slow growing smile. "You strike me as someone who is great at everything."

Cindy unpacked a mixer, several bowls, spoons and containers of flour and sugar, setting them all on the counter.

"For someone who isn't good at baking, it looks like you plan to do a lot of it."

She sighed. "Every Christmas I try to improve by making a few recipes from a list of the hardest desserts to make."

He laughed again. "I had no idea you were so competitive."

"It's become a family joke, like your whipped cream. Although I'm the butt of the joke. Here…" She walked to another box, pulled out several aprons, and flopped them over the back of a dining chair. "These aprons were all given to me by my older brothers."

Rafe picked up the aprons one-by-one reading the words out loud.

I'm sexy sweet with a naughty center.
Well, butter my buns n' call me a biscuit.
This girl rubs her meat before she sticks it in.
Sugar Slut.

"Your brothers gave you this one too?" He held up a red and white polka-dot pinup-girl style apron.

"Oh God." Cindy grabbed it and held it behind her back. "No."

He lifted an eyebrow.

"That's…no." She studied the way he pursed his lips trying not to laugh. "Go ahead, you can say what you're thinking."

His mouth tilted up on one side in a mischievous smirk.

She raised her eyes to the ceiling. "I know what you're thinking anyway."

"No." He shook his head. "I don't believe that you do."

Lifting her chin, she brought the apron out from behind her back and flapped it to straighten the material. "I like it. Maybe it's a little silly. I wear it for special occasions."

He nodded. "That would be special."

Heat crept across her cheeks. "Stop. It's an apron."

He chuckled. "What are you making this year?"

She threw the red apron on top of the others and continued unloading supplies.

"Well, key lime pie is tomorrow. Then a wedding cake so I can practice my decorating skills."

"Wow, and then you eat all that too?"

She scrunched her face at him. "Of course not. I'd be big as a house. Besides, my desserts are typically inedible." She shrugged. "I keep trying."

Rafe picked up the tubs filled with Christmas decorations, moving them to the far side of the living room by the window. "Do you only practice baking once a year? Maybe that's part of the issue."

Cindy laughed. "You could be right. Hey, what do you think of the tree?"

"I was going to ask who put a live tree in here."

"I arranged it in advance with Mr. Clack."

"Who's that?"

"The owner. You've been here. I'm sure you've met him before."

"Do you mean Jack?" Rafe cracked up as he walked back to the kitchen. "His name is Jack Clack?"

She laughed with him. "Yes, how unfortunate."

"Now, that's funny." He leaned on the counter that separated the small dining area from the kitchen. "Okay with you if I have one of those beers you mentioned?"

She closed the fridge, opened one of the coolers and handed him a bottle. "Of course. Let's put the game on too. I had Jack Clack," she snickered, "set it to record so I had something to watch tonight. I'm allowed an evening of relaxation because tomorrow it's all revising, decorating the tree, and baking."

She opened her own beer, took a sip, and set it on the counter as Rafe walked to the living room.

She enjoyed Rafe and their new friendship since she moved back to Ashnee Valley a year ago. Easy-going and confident, he'd impressed her with his natural intuitiveness about the mutual friends they had in town and their recent troubles. It didn't escape her when he flubbed his words around her and especially the way her pulse surged in reaction. Way over six feet tall, with a sexy beard and handsome. Plus, built like a rock. There was no other way to see him than utterly masculine.

She peeked around the corner as he stood in front of the TV, his back to her.

Camo pants.

Nice to see a great rear-end in something other

than the boring saggy-bottom khakis her male psychiatry colleagues seemed so attached to.

"I found it." Rafe said turning around.

She lifted her beer to her lips to hide any impropriety at staring.

"Great. I'm almost done in here. Would you like some popcorn or your pork rinds? I could make you a sandwich."

He walked her direction and put his hands flat on the counter.

"You don't need to fuss over me," he said. "I'm the one imposing on your space. If I wasn't here, what would you be doing right now?"

She turned on the gas stove and put a Jiffy-Pop on the burner, holding the handle with a potholder.

"I'd do this. Have a drink, watch the game, eat popcorn, wear my fuzzy pajamas."

Rafe shrugged. "So do that. Don't let me get in the way." He came farther into the kitchen. "I'll take over popcorn duty while you go do the pajama thing."

"They have feet."

"What has feet?"

"My fuzzy pajamas."

He shook the popcorn as it began to pop but didn't respond, a tiny smile on his lips.

"Do you wear pajamas?" She put her hand up, laughing off her awkward question. "Okay, that was completely weird. Sorry. I just ...I might feel more comfortable if it's not just me wearing pajamas."

He moved the popcorn from the burner, turned

off the stove, and faced her.

"Do I make you nervous? Because I don't want to be doing that."

"No, not at all." Cindy swiped a hand in the air. "I'm having fun. And no, you don't make me nervous. Do I make you nervous?" She dropped her shoulders with a self-conscious wince. "I tend to make men nervous."

Rafe rubbed his hand on the back of his neck as he spoke. "I can understand how you might make some men nervous. A certain type of man." He tipped his head to the side. "The type of man who isn't comfortable in the company of an intelligent, beautiful woman."

She inhaled and held her breath.

He rubbed his thumb at the corner of his bottom lip. "I'm not that kind of guy."

"Yes, well…" She quietly exhaled as she studied her hands, picking at her cuticles. "Good," she said lifting her gaze to his. "Because I can appear pretty intimidating in my footy pajamas."

"I'll keep that in mind." He chuckled.

She scrunched her nose. "Sometimes it does seem to me like I fluster you. A little."

He glanced her way then opened several cupboard doors before finding a large bowl for the popcorn.

"Oh, flustered." He drew the words out in an exaggerated way. "You've noticed the tongue-tied thing, eh?"

"Maybe."

"That's different than intimidated." He fixed his blue eyes on her. "You make me want to keep up with you. It's a feeling I like. Even if I trip over myself."

"Ah, okay, so it's like eagerness or enthusiasm."

His laughter boomed forth. "Sure. We can call it that."

She lifted a shoulder with a knowing smile. "It hasn't really happened much since we got to the cabin I've noticed."

"Huh. You're right," he answered. "Let's see how I do once you break out those pajamas."

She delighted in the buoyant flirty bounce of her heart. "I'll meet you at the couch in five minutes."

Chapter 3

Rafe usually slept naked, but that clearly wasn't the plan for tonight. Lifting his duffel bag onto the couch, he dug through it until he found a pair of navy-blue sweatpants. It wasn't pajamas but seemed the least he could do. Stepping into the bathroom he switched out his pants and pulled a well-worn orange sweatshirt over his head then walked back to the kitchen.

He put the popcorn into the bowl, downed the rest of his beer, then reached into the fridge for another. Out of the corner of his eye, he saw Cindy return to the living room.

"It's the half." She spoke over the back of the couch. "I guess we could rewind, but no one has scored. Should we just keep going?"

He carried the snack bowl into the room setting it on the cushion between them before taking a seat. "Yeah, it's already eleven. Doesn't look like there's much to this game." He set the book he planned to start reading on the end table beside him.

Cindy fast-forwarded to the end of the half and hit play but left the TV on mute. "What are you reading?"

"I haven't started it yet." He handed the book to her. "It's about Achilles. It's on the best-seller list."

"I've heard of this," she said reading the blurb on the back. "Do you like Greek mythology?"

"I do." He stuffed a handful of popcorn in his mouth. "I read anything good, though. I like World War Two history—and horror."

She shook her shoulders. "Horror, not me. I haven't read anything for fun since I started writing my second book. I can't wait for it to be finished."

"What made you decide to write a book on intimacy?"

She raised her eyebrows. "I'm surprised you know the topic."

"You mentioned it this fall when we had lunch with Jim Mannis at Café Lilly. It's pretty different from your first book."

Cindy tucked her pajama-covered feet under her, pulled an afghan from the back of the couch over her lap, and shifted to face his direction.

"My first book was about dealing with the grief of my twin sister's death a long time ago."

"I'm sorry that happened to you," he said. "I read it."

She wrinkled her nose. "You did? I'm surprised. It's not exactly uplifting."

He smiled. "I don't have any brothers or sisters. But it made me think about Jim. We're Army buddies, but he's more like a brother to me. I bet your book helped a lot of people."

She nodded. "It did well. Anyway, as for the current book, over the years in my practice, I've found a lot of my clients have no grasp of physical progression in their relationships. Granted, most of them are inexperienced or socially challenged in one way or another."

She took a handful of popcorn, eating one piece at a time. "This book is less research focused. I hope I don't get lambasted when it's reviewed."

Rafe took a swig of his beer. "Why would that happen?"

"Physical progress toward intimacy is fairly simple. So, in some ways the book is simple, like a step-by-step guide. To me, it's intended for a certain audience. I've had a few go-rounds with the publisher who wants to market the book to a broader constituency. I hope it doesn't come off like a cheesy magazine article. Ten steps to get laid or whatever. You wouldn't believe the fight we've had about the cover."

"Tell me that part. What'd they want to put on the cover?"

Cindy rolled her eyes. "A ladder, which I guess someone thought was original."

He dipped his chin. "Just a ladder?"

"I wish. At the top of the ladder, they put a woman in a skirt. At the bottom of the ladder is a man." She gave him a dead-pan look. "Doing who knows what. Looking up her skirt, I guess."

He snorted. "What step of the progression is that?"

"Step six." She laughed. "I'm kidding. It's not. Being a pervert who looks up women's skirts is not included."

He put his hand out. "Give me the remote." When she slapped the device into his palm, he turned off the game, which still hovered at zero to zero.

"I want to hear the steps," he said with a devilish grin.

"See." Cindy cringed. "I'm afraid the book won't be taken seriously. It will all be jokes about getting to third base or home plate."

"There's baseball in it too?" He gaped in mock-astonishment. "It sounds better and better, the more you talk about it."

She put a hand on his upper arm and gently shoved. "Stop. You're witnessing the part where every writer freaks out before their book is published."

"I wouldn't worry. Your first book did well. You've been in practice for what, twenty-something years? You'll be taken seriously. So, what are the steps?"

Cindy stood for a quick moment to wrap the afghan around her shoulders then settled back on the couch.

"You and I have probably done the early steps already."

Rafe wiggled his eyebrows. "Really?"

She laughed. "Number one is eye to body; two, eye to eye; three, voice to voice; four is hand to hand. Five and six are often together – they're arm to shoulder and arm to waist. Seven and eight are often together as well, mouth to mouth and hand to head. Nine is hand to body. Ten is mouth to torso and eleven is an act of final culmination."

He flashed a silly grin. "Final culmination. Is that what the kids call it these days?"

"Yes," she said. "You can't just assume what that means exactly."

He dipped his chin. "Uh, yeah, you can."

"I mean, it doesn't presume a particular position." She waved her hand in the air. "So, to speak."

He squinted, furrowing his brow as he struggled to maintain a serious expression.

"See! That, right there. That look on your face. That's my fear."

"I'm teasing you. Culmination doesn't sound like it presumes other things either. It doesn't have to mean only male and female couples, or only young couples, for example. The absence of being specific is a plus."

"Do you think so? That's what I hope."

"Of course. I see what you're saying too. During this evening, we've done steps one, two and three already."

"Right." She picked up the bowl and set it on her lap. "You can see where people could get into real trouble if they skip steps or do them completely out of order. They could scare the heck out of another person. Again, I'm not talking about people who are experienced already."

Rafe nodded. "I think your book is going to do very well just like the first one. It will help many people."

"Thank you." Cindy passed the popcorn bowl to him. "Want to see if anyone ever scored in this game?"

"Yeah, one question first." A thoughtful squint crinkled the corners of his eyes. "When's the last time you did all the steps?"

"Excuse me?" she said with a bemused blink.

"Whew." He blew out a breath. "I didn't ask that correctly." He paused to collect his thoughts. "It strikes me that a lot of people wouldn't do all the steps. Isn't a one-night-stand just skipping right to culmination?"

"No, actually most couples don't skip the steps. They aren't aware they're following them naturally and pretty much in order. Even if they blast through them in ten minutes in a race to get to the finish line."

"Maybe it should be a guide for everyone then," he said.

"I get your drift. Sex in the modern day can be rather perfunctory."

He debated pressing that button or whether to back out with a stretch of his arms and yawn indicating he was ready to sleep.

"Perfunctory?" he asked after a brief pause.

"It means without effort." Cindy said.

He laughed. "I know what the word means. Would you care to elaborate?"

She breathed in and out through her nose. "Are you sure you'd like to hear the answer?"

He shook his head, purposely contradicting the words coming out of his mouth. "Yes, I'm sure."

She closed her eyes and scratched her scalp.

"Perfunctory," she repeated the word, sounding as if this were a spelling bee, "to me, is when you don't have a relationship *per se*, but you have sex with someone for convenience, just basic meeting of physical needs. There's no curiosity to it. No discovery. No passion." Her eyes widened. "Frankly, it's a bore. And you know what?"

He tilted his head, wary of the teeny, tiny wobble to her voice.

"Perfunctory isn't even friends with benefits. We were never friends." She lifted her chin. "Sorry. I just had a flashback to a prior relationship that ended poorly."

Rafe set the popcorn bowl on the coffee table and took her hand.

"Hey, Cyn." He liked the fact that she didn't let go. He paused before he spoke again.

"I don't know if I suffer so much from perfunctory as much as attracting the wrong age group."

"What do you mean?"

He shrugged. "Are you sure you'd like to hear the answer?"

"Yes." She mimicked his earlier response by shaking her head with a smirk.

He stroked his thumb once along the back of her hand with a chuckle. "A lot of younger women find me very attractive."

A snort laugh escaped, and Cindy slapped her other hand over her mouth. "I'm so sorry, that was rude of me. How young?"

"Twenties. I mean, look at me. I'm in my forties. I work out regularly. I'm tall."

Cindy's hand tightened around his when

another giggle erupted. "Sorry." She shook her head. "Please continue."

He fixed his eyes on hers then shot her a flirtatious wink. "I'm extremely good-looking."

"Yes, I can see the dilemma." Her lip quivered. "It must be so terrible for you."

He tugged her hand and pulled her playfully toward him. "Don't laugh. Twenty is too young. It creeps me out."

"Okay, let's be serious here. Besides the obvious, why do you think women half your age like you so much?"

He let go her hand and moved his arm to the back of the couch. "They're looking for a protector or a financial provider. Who knows."

"Hmm. Yes, it probably is primal in the physical ways you first described, but I can see how it would include confidence and being mature emotionally as well," Cindy said. "I've never attracted younger men."

"I doubt that's accurate. You just didn't realize it."

"No, I attract a certain kind of practical, older, professional man. Where you get the hot twenty-somethings, I get the fifty to sixty-year-old demographic. A lot of times they're married, which is disturbing. Men don't see me as someone to share a life with. I'm too driven. Never spontaneous enough."

Rafe squeezed her shoulder. "Okay, this conversation is starting to go downhill."

Cindy sat up and put her hands on her cheeks. "You're right. It's getting late anyway." She folded the afghan before putting it on the back of the couch. "We both need sleep."

She picked up the popcorn bowl and walked toward the kitchen.

"Are you thinking what I'm thinking?" he asked as he spread a blanket on the couch and put the pillow at one end.

Cindy walked through the living room then stopped at the doorway to her bedroom. "About how we just blew through step four? Hand to hand? Never crossed my mind. Goodnight, Rafe."

"Goodnight, Cindy."

Chapter 4

CINDY ROSE EARLY, TIPTOEING IN the early morning darkness past Rafe who snored softly on the couch. In the kitchen she turned on the light above the stove and started the coffee maker.

At the small dining table, she set out her laptop, papers, references, a variety of different colored notepads and some pens. How she loved a good office supply store, spending an hour wandering the aisles of endless organizational tools.

That reminded her, she'd brought a giant flip board chart. Looking around, she found it leaning against the wall by the front door. The board would come in handy later in the day as part of her baking time since one challenge was forgetting a key ingredient. It worked better when she wrote all the ingredients in large print on the board and crossed them off the list as she went. Who'd want a key lime pie without the lime flavor?

A couple hours later her phone rang and Rafe

awoke at the sound with a loud snort.

"What's happening?" He sat up and rubbed his eyes.

She held up an index finger as she answered her phone.

"Hello. This is Cindy. Good morning, Mr. Clack. I'm fine. How are you?" She paused, listening for a moment as she watched Rafe run his fingers through his hair in the most rumply male way. "That bad, huh?"

He turned to her with a questioning look.

"I see," she said, holding eye contact with Rafe. "How long are they saying it will take to clear the canyon road? Yes, twenty-six inches up here is a lot even for Hawkeye. No, I'm fine."

Rafe yawned and carefully folded his sheet and blanket as he listened.

"I have everything I need right here. Thank you, Mr. Clack. Say hi to Sylvia for me. I appreciate that. Yes, keep me updated. Thanks for calling. Mmm hmm. Okay, goodbye."

"What'd he say?"

"It's possible they'll have the road cleared sometime overnight." She bit her bottom lip. "There's more snow in the forecast though. Not a lot more, but it could slow them down. So, it might be late tomorrow, he says."

"If it takes that long, I won't be leaving here until Christmas morning."

She winced in sympathy at the worried expression on his face. "I'm so sorry. This is my fault."

"How is it your fault? You said you can't control the weather."

"I wish I could. Your parents will be so disappointed."

As he stretched, his t-shirt lifted above the waistband of his sweats. She grabbed her coffee mug as she checked out his taut muscles on display. She took a big swallow of air from her empty mug and still managed to choke.

"They'll be fine. I spent so many years in the Army away from home for the holidays that they don't care when I show up, just that I come visit."

She smiled. "That's sweet. My mother is the same way."

"Besides," he said as he stacked his pillow and blankets neatly on a chair, "I'm the one putting you out for longer. Am I going to mess with your book work by being here? I'll be quiet."

She chuckled softly. "No. I hope it won't be too boring though. I do have to work this morning. I'm not good at writing with background noise unfortunately."

Rafe put up a hand. "Say no more. I'll take a shower and start reading. Later, I'll see if I can shovel my way to my truck."

"Okay." She tilted her head. "There's coffee if you want some. I don't really have any breakfast foods other than bread for toast. Sorry."

"What time did you get up?"

"Let's see." She glanced at her phone again. "It's eight. About three hours ago."

Rafe dipped his chin. "Five?"

"I'm spending eight hours on my writing. That will put me at one o'clock. Then I'm making key lime pie. After that I decorate the tree."

Rafe picked up his duffel bag from the corner of the room and set it on the floor next the bathroom. "Is key lime pie on the list of difficult desserts?"

"Yes. It's the meringue that's tricky." She pointed to her flip chart. "There aren't all that many ingredients."

He walked to her chart and read through the pie instructions. "Do you always write out the recipes on a big board?"

"I do," she said, deciding not to explain further at seeing the smirk on his face.

He nodded, then walked to the kitchen, took a mug from the cupboard, poured coffee for himself, and returned.

"Sounds delicious. It's one of my favorites," he said. "Although I can't think of a type of pie I don't like."

"Oh, good." She put a hand to her heart. "That's a relief. I don't actually like key lime pie."

Rafe's laugh boomed through the room. "What? That makes no sense. Why are you making it then?"

"I told you." She got up and went to the kitchen to refill her coffee. "It's on the list."

"Yeah, but what's the point if the outcome is something you don't even want?" He stared at her wide-eyed.

Cindy sat at the table again. "That's part of the challenge."

With a shrug, Rafe walked to the bathroom.

At the sound of the shower starting, Cindy glanced at the manuscript on her laptop then picked up her cell phone to skim through her emails. Surprised at seeing one from the university she'd recently interviewed with, she inhaled.

I'm sure they wanted to get the rejection out the door before the holidays.

"Dr. Wheeler," she read. "We're pleased to extend an invitation for you to join the faculty in the Department of Psychiatry at Boston University. All who met you during your interviews were extremely impressed with your credentials and successful years in practice. Attached is our formal offer. If you have any questions or wish to discuss more, please let us know. We would like to fill the position immediately. We hope to hear from you with your answer prior to the start of the new year."

Cindy put a hand over her beating heart. *Oh my God. Boston. The new year. That's only a few days.*

After a short time, the bathroom door opened and Rafe stepped out. She glanced up, shaken loose from staring out the window at the snow.

He wore jeans and a gray long-sleeve t-shirt that said Army in big black letters on it. He walked by the table barefoot toward the kitchen.

She glimpsed down at her own outfit with a frown. She wasn't in her usual pantsuit ensemble for work, but still managed to be oddly formal in her designer casual wear with matching house slippers.

The toaster popped in the kitchen, followed by the scrape of a knife spreading butter on toast. She kept her head bent as Rafe walked by the table again, plate and mug in hand, and settled on the couch.

With his back to her, she lifted her gaze, studying him as he picked up his book. *He's a reader.* Cindy rested her chin on her hand. *That is so undeniably sexy.*

He fluffed one of the pillows with a sudden glance her direction.

"Caught you drifting," he said with a smile lifting the corner of his mouth. "Get to work."

She nodded and began typing immediately then paused to read the words she wrote.

What's the point if the outcome is something you don't even want?

A second cup of coffee, one bathroom trip, and three hours later, she'd reached her limit with revising her manuscript.

Rafe had managed to push the snow at the front door enough to get out on the porch to shovel. Snow had started again and when she glanced out the front window, what little progress he made became quickly covered with a new layer. She watched him working for another minute before moving the flip chart to the kitchen and propping it against the side of the fridge.

After laying out all the ingredients, she began on the pie crust, pleased when this came along more easily than she expected. She pricked the bottom several times with a fork then moved on to preparing the filling, heating it on the stove. When ready, she poured it into the pie crust and put the whole thing in the oven.

That wasn't so bad.

The cabin door opened and Rafe came inside

stomping his feet on the mat while brushing snow from his coat.

She put a towel on the floor near the door. "For wet items. How'd it go out there?"

He brushed frozen clumps of snow from his hat before tossing it on the towel.

"I got to my truck. I think the fuel line is frozen. Not sure I'd be going anywhere anyway even without the snow."

"Hopefully, the temperatures will come up with the sun out."

She walked back to the kitchen. "I decided to get started on the baking a little earlier. The pie is already in the oven. Time to start the meringue."

"You already baked the crust and have the whole pie already back in there? That was fast."

She pressed her lips together and quickly consulted her chart, reading through the ingredients accounting for each one.

"Yes," she answered with a confident nod, then turned away and opened the fridge, hiding her expression of dread behind the door.

Pre-bake the crust?

"Sounds like it's going great." He walked farther into the kitchen. "Can you hand me a beer please?"

"Sure." She reached in the fridge. "Here."

"Unless you want some help, I'll go back to my book." He grabbed the bag of pork rinds.

Cindy studied the cookbook on how to separate the yolks from the whites. Not even a speck of yolk can remain, the recipe cheerfully taunted.

"I'm sorry, what?"

"Unless you want some help," he repeated, "I'll go back to my book."

"That's fine. I'm good." She beamed a fake smile to cover the looming failure of yet another soggy pie crust.

"How long does the pie have to cool before we can try it?" he asked.

"Oh, um…" Flustered, she dropped an egg, shell, and all, into the bowl in front of her. "Four hours."

Rafe chuckled. "Guess that one's a loss," he said and left the room.

After fifteen minutes her meringue recovered from the soggy droopy stage and formed peaks. With potholder mitts she lifted the glass pie plate to examine the seepy bottom crust. She glopped the meringue on top foregoing any attempt at artfulness now that her interest waned, knowing it was a failure. Sticking the pie back in the oven, she allowed the door to bang shut of its own volition and set the timer.

"Drat," she mumbled and turned. "Oh!" She put a hand to her chest at finding Rafe leaning on the counter watching her. "You scared me."

"I didn't mean to. How's the pie?"

"It needs a few more minutes. May I help you with something?"

She narrowed her eyes at his mischievous expression as if daring him to call her out for her slightly prissy tone.

"I thought I could get started on the lights for the tree. That's usually the hardest part."

"That would be very helpful. Thank you."

"Are you sure everything is okay in here?" he asked with a knowing smirk.

"Yes. I'll meet you at the tree in a few minutes." She made sure he left the room before opening the oven door for a peek. Then waited, arms crossed, swallowing defeat while the timer counted down.

Seriously, why can I not do this?

Chapter 5

Rafe opened the plastic tub labeled X-mas lights and smiled at the neatly organized strands fastened with large twist-ties. No untangling to do. He softly laughed. *I may be in love.*

"What's so funny?" Cindy said, walking around the couch to take a seat.

"You." He smiled. "This is the most organized box of lights I've ever seen."

"There's an extension cord in there too," she noted.

"Hey." He sat down next to her with a playful bump of his shoulder to hers. "You've been working hard all day. How about I string the lights on the tree and then make us dinner while you put the ornaments on? I make a mean grilled ham and cheese. It looked like everything needed for that is in the fridge."

She peered up at him from under her long lashes. "Yes, please."

His gaze settled on the cute-as-hell pout on

her lips.

"Don't do that, Rafe Mooney," she said with a bump now to his shoulder.

His eyes flicked to hers again. "What?"

"Look like you might want to kiss a vulnerable woman who can't even make a pie."

He chuckled as he put his arm around her shoulder. "Do you want to tell me what went wrong now, or do we try the pie later and discuss it then?"

She laughed while snuggling closer. "Later," she mumbled and laid her head on his shoulder. "I need to redeem myself first by decorating a beautiful tree."

He squeezed her arm, let go, and stood. "Got it."

He walked to the kitchen, grabbed two beers, came back in the room, and handed one to her. "Here. It's five o'clock somewhere. Want to put some music on while I get started?"

She took a sip and smiled fondly at him. "Are you always this easy going?"

"Pretty much," he answered as he dug out the cord from the bottom of the box. "I'm a simple guy, Cyn. At least since I left the military." He shrugged. "You only live once. Might as well have a good time."

"Mmm." She walked to the stereo and sat on the floor in front of a row of albums on the lower shelf underneath the turntable. "When's the last time you listened to music on vinyl?"

"It's been a while. Anything good there?"

"Well, there's holiday music if we want to go

that route. Ooh, Chicago. Oh, here we go…" she giggled… "Kiss."

"Go for it," he said and untied a string of lights.

She put the record on and sat back on the couch. After one song, she walked back to the turntable and lifted the needle.

"Done with that?" He chuckled as he circled the tree.

"Yes." She switched out records for a familiar Fleetwood Mac album instead.

He stopped for a moment to take a swallow of beer. "Good choice."

"So, what are your plans once the buildout of Mercy Mountain Lodge is finished?" she asked.

He continued wrapping lights around the tree, considering the conclusion of the construction work he'd been doing over the past year for the new vacation resort in Ashnee Valley.

"The Mannises want the cottages ready for reservations by spring. What's left is putting in the mechanicals. I'm pretty much done with my part there now." He untied another string as he spoke. "Plus, I have well overstayed my welcome living at Jim and Sofia's house." He rolled his eyes. "They're still like newlyweds and there I am in the middle of that."

"Are you going to move back to New Mexico?"

"Funny you should ask." He took a break to sit on the couch again, reaching in the box of lights. "No. I'm staying in Ashnee Valley." He glanced at her. "I was just offered a coaching position at the high school."

Cindy beamed. "Congratulations. Football?"

"Nope. Biathlon. Rifle and cross-country ski coach."

"I had no idea they had such a program there."

"Yep. It's part-time to start. I'm trying to convince the high school in Four Bears to add it to their sports roster too. I told them I could go back and forth a couple days at each location every week if they do." He got up and started on the tree again. "I'm not sure they can come up with the funding, but why not ask?"

"That's a great idea. Sounds like you planted the seed with them at least. Will you be coaching boys or girls?"

"Both. But you know who's a natural born athlete? That girl that hangs out with Kai Mannis's kids all the time. Nicki. She's already a cross-country running champ in the state. She's the best shot I've seen in someone who basically just started training. We'll see how her skiing goes."

"I know her family," Cindy added. "Nicki's mother is a seasonal worker at one of the big shipping companies. She's gone for months at a time, so Nicki and her older brother are often on their own. I'm sure that's why she hangs out with the Mannis family so much. It's unfortunate about her stepfather's situation."

Rafe scoffed. "Situation? You mean jail. He's a dirtbag." He glanced at her wary expression. "Am I wrong?"

Cindy sighed. "He's trouble."

"All the more reason she needs positive influences, like sports. Okay, here goes nothing." He bent to plug the extension cord into the wall outlet, and the lights on the tree flickered to life.

"Oh, that's lovely. I love the holidays." Cindy walked to the tree. "It looks fantastic."

"Thanks." Rafe rubbed his hands together. "I'm starving. Do you want one or two sandwiches?"

She chuckled. "One is fine for me. I'll decorate fast so we can eat." She glanced around the room. "I'll need to stand on something when I get to the angel that goes on top."

"I'll do that part," he called over his shoulder as he walked to the kitchen to get dinner started.

From the kitchen he listened to the second side of the album on the stereo. He opened the fridge, heartbroken at the fortress of cardboard Cindy had built around her key lime pie to hide it from view.

If she thinks I wanted to kiss her before, just wait until she reveals this hidden disaster. The woman tries too damn hard.

Surprised to find only one small frying pan, he set to work preparing one grilled sandwich at a time and keeping them warm in the oven as he went.

Twenty minutes later, he put the last foil wrapped sandwich on a cookie sheet when he heard a loud thud and yelp.

Rushing toward the living room, he took in Cindy's frown as she held the back of a chair next to the tree and stood on one leg.

"What happened? Are you okay?"

"I wanted to put the angel on top so the tree would be all finished." She gave him a sheepish look and tried to put weight on her foot, wincing. "I must have landed funny when I stepped down off the chair."

"Hold on." He swept her into his arms and carried her the three feet to the couch. He sat down with her on his lap and leaned back.

"I told you I'd do that part." He kept his arms around her.

"I know." She offered in an apologetic tone. "I think it's just a little sprain."

"Not a full break?" he asked sarcastically. "Maybe you didn't try hard enough then."

"Stop." She laughed with a swat to his arm. "This day…"

Rafe rubbed her back, then tightened his arms around her. "You need to look at things differently. Stop trying so hard to be perfect. I've had a great day being around you. That's how I see it."

She nodded before gingerly moving off his lap without bumping her foot. "You're right."

Coaxing her to turn he lifted her leg across his knees and examined her ankle. "Can you move it?"

She turned her foot slowly side to side, then up and down. "It hurts when I do that. I'll be okay."

She glanced at the tree. "The angel looks good though."

He smiled and shook his head. "You stay. Don't move. Got it? I'll bring our sandwiches and ice for your ankle." He handed her the remote. "Here. You find us a movie."

It was after the movie when he could see out the big window in the living room that it was snowing hard again.

"I think you're going to be stuck with me another day," he said pointing and then put his arm along the back of the couch.

"Oh, shucks," Cindy said with a shy smile and tugged his hand, so his arm came around her shoulders.

"Don't do that, Cindy Wheeler," he said to tease.

She pressed her lips together. "What?"

"Encourage a seriously flustered man with steps five and six."

"Arm to shoulder, arm to waist. I'm impressed you remember."

They stared at each other for so long he thought his heart would pop out of his chest.

"Well, you'll have to suck it up and do it again a couple more times." She lifted her chin. "It's time you carry me to the kitchen so we can eat my terrible pie, and then you can carry me to my bedroom."

He wiggled his eyebrows. A pretty pink flush spread across her cheeks.

"So, I can sleep," she dead panned.

He chuckled and sat forward on the couch. With an arm around her back and the other under her knees, he lifted her, walked to the kitchen, and set her on the counter. He opened the utensil drawer and handed her two forks. Then he removed the cardboard fort from the refrigerator and put the pie plate next to her.

"You first," he said with a smirk.

"Aren't you going to cut slices?"

He shook his head. "We're going to be spontaneous and just stick our forks in the middle." He tipped his head toward the dessert. "Go."

"Very well." She stabbed her fork in the center and scooped out a bite.

He glanced at the pie plate. "The crust is still in there."

"That's right. See, I'm not perfect," she said around a mouthful. "Your turn."

Rafe scooped a giant forkful, held it up to her with a nod, and shoved it into his mouth. A burst of lime hit his taste buds. Too much lime. He squeezed his eyes closed with an all over body shiver.

"Whew!" he said with a whip of his head. "That is seriously sour."

Cindy cracked up as he put his hands on her knees, standing close to the counter.

"Back to the couch for a bit, or bedtime?" he asked.

She smiled. "I'm getting up early again to work on my book."

"Okay, wrap your arms and legs around me." His eyes flicked to hers apprehensive at what reaction he'd get to his presumptuous suggestion.

She put her arms around his neck. "I'm spent."

Rafe picked her up, careful to avoid bumping her ankle. "Bed it is," he said and carried her to her room.

Chapter 6

AFTER PROPPING HER ANKLE ON a pillow and setting two aspirin and a glass of water on the bedside table, Rafe said goodnight and left her alone.

Cindy got out her reading glasses, but instead of putting them on, she bit the stem.

Is cringy-worthy embarrassment and lust possible to feel simultaneously?

She picked up her phone, squinting at a text from Mr. Clack she'd missed two hours ago. She put on her glasses again and read his note saying Dark Horse Canyon remained closed. She then re-read the offer email from Boston University.

Moving carefully, she stood and hobbled to the tiny half-bath off her bedroom and put on her pajamas and brushed her teeth. She sat on the edge of the bed again, took the aspirin, and turned off the bedside light.

The low murmur and glowing light from the TV in the living room flickered beneath the door. Cindy lay back and clasped her hands on her chest. She blinked several times, waiting for her eyes to adjust to the darkness.

She revisited the way her body had thrummed with blissful pleasure when Rafe carried her to bed. She shook her head and reached in the darkness for her eyeglasses on the table. Picking up her phone she opened a notes app to make a quick list.

'Number one', she typed followed by the words, 'manuscript work.'

Those piercing blue eyes.

She typed 'number two' then, 'decide whether to take job in Boston.'

Strong arms. Killer bum.

Her cell phone landed with a painful thud, hitting the edge of her chin when she dropped it to her chest.

She picked her phone up again. 'Number three', she added to the list, 'help me.'

When the light went out in the other room, Cindy quickly held her phone to her chest to extinguish the glow. She held her breath as if Rafe might hear her rapid heartbeat.

In the gray light of early morning, after a fitful night of sleep, Cindy awoke to a stiff, achy ankle. She turned on the bedside lamp and rested on her elbow while she slipped the fuzzy sock off her swollen foot. It now sported a good size purple bruise.

Merry Christmas Eve.

She pushed herself higher in bed and leaned on the headboard. She lifted her lap desk from where it rested against the side of the bed, set her laptop on it, and began working.

Four hours later, she listened to Rafe answering a knock at the front door and speaking with Mr. Clack although she couldn't make out what they were saying. The roads must be better if he came in person to give an update.

She hobbled to the bathroom, collected her items for a shower, and opened her bedroom door.

"Good morning."

"Hey." Rafe glanced up from reading on the couch. "I was wondering if you were up. I thought you'd be at the table working already."

"I was sitting up in bed working. I'm going to take a shower."

He glanced at her foot. "How's your ankle doing?"

She stuck out her leg for him to see. "I can put pressure on it and the swelling has gone way down. Just a pretty purple color now."

"That's good. I'll feel better about leaving, knowing you're able to get around okay."

Drat.

"So, the roads are clear?"

"They will be by later tonight. That was Jack at the door a few minutes ago. I was able to start my truck too. If you can stand it, I'll head out tomorrow. It's an eleven-hour drive to my folks' place. If I leave early enough, I can be there for Christmas dinner."

"Of course," she said with a smile. "That's great. Have you called and told them you'll be on your way?"

"I'll do that now. I didn't want to wake you in case you were sleeping. Are you hungry?" he asked. "I was about to make myself some lunch."

Her stomach growled in response to his suggestion.

"I guess I am. Lunch would be great." She carefully walked to the bathroom and shut the door, eavesdropping when she heard him speaking.

"Hey, it's me. Good news, the weather has let up and the roads are being cleared. I should be there by suppertime tomorrow." He laughed at something. "Tell Mom not to expect me to be clean cut. I know. I was going to get a haircut before I came to the house." He chuckled again. "She loves me. She'll survive. You can prepare her for the shaggy version. Yep, I'll see you tomorrow. Love you, Dad. Bye."

Cindy started the shower.

The least I can do is offer him a haircut.

She emerged from the steamy bathroom twenty minutes later and returned to her room for a few minutes before joining Rafe in the kitchen.

"Do you want mayo on your sandwich?" he asked.

"Yes. Um, so I wasn't really trying to listen to your phone call earlier, but I did. Would you like a haircut?"

He glanced over his shoulder wide-eyed. "Me?"

Cindy looked around the room as if searching for another person. "Yes, you." She held up her index finger. "Wait, before I go further, hold on."

She left the kitchen to rummage through her box of office supplies and returned holding up a small black case.

"I have scissors."

He chuckled. "That's okay, but thanks."

She tipped her head to the side. "Scared?"

"No." He carried a plate in each hand to the small dining table and gestured for her to take a seat. He brought a napkin and a glass of water for her, then sat down.

"I know what I'm doing. I worked at a salon during college to help pay for my undergrad degree."

"You did?"

She nodded. "I could clean things up a little. Just a trim." She lifted a shoulder. "My Christmas present for your mom."

He took a bite of his sandwich. "All right. After lunch."

"Good." She sat up straight. "This will be fun. Besides what else is there to do? I can't bake the cake I planned today."

His eyes lifted again. "The one with frosting?"

She smirked. "Yes, but knowing me, it would come out like a shellacked brick."

"You like cake with frosting though, right?"

She took a bite of her sandwich and nodded.

"Well, we're making some progress then. I could make it."

"You?" She gaped.

"Scared?"

"Touché," she laughed and looked down at her

plate.

"Cyn, what's the matter? I can tell something is bothering you. You've been hidden in your room half the day. That's not like you."

She lifted her eyes to his. "I have to make a decision. It's a big one."

He put his sandwich down and pushed his plate forward. "Okay."

She ran her fingers along the edges of her placemat straightening the fringe. "I have a job offer from Boston University in their Psychiatry Department." She sighed. "I applied months ago, then didn't hear much after. It's a surprise. It could be the next logical step in my career, if I don't start my own practice, but…"

"But what?" he asked after a long pause.

She didn't have the courage to say her thoughts out loud. *That's so far from everyone. From Colorado. I'd miss you.* "The East Coast is far away."

"It is," he agreed. "How soon?"

She dropped her shoulders. "They want an answer before the end of the year."

"Hey," he said, "why the long face? This is big. You deserve it, Cindy. I don't know anyone that works as hard as you."

"Thank you." She swallowed the lump in her throat. "I have a lot to think about."

He picked up his plate and walked to the kitchen. "The good news is I'll be out of your way soon."

She picked up her sandwich then set it down again. "Sure," she said, sensing his fast departure from the table was only the beginning of his withdraw.

I wish I hadn't said anything.

"I changed my mind," Rafe called from the kitchen. "I'm going to make the cake now. You should rest your ankle anyway." He returned to the table with an apron in each hand. "Which is more me? Naughty center or sugar slut?"

She laughed despite feeling all her energy drain from her body. Weakened, she pushed her plate to the side and put her forehead on the table.

"Ugh. I don't know what to do."

"Cyn." He ran his hand along her hair. "Give yourself time."

She wanted to wrap her arms around his legs as he stood next to her chair to hold him in place forever.

Why? Why this job now? Why this man making me want to chuck everything and just…I don't know.

"You'll know what you want." Rafe patted her back. "The decision will come to you."

With her head still resting on the table she rolled her eyes.

A pat on the back. Nice going, Cindy. You sure have a way of cutting a man off at the knees.

"I'm going to get started. We'll see if there's time for a haircut later," he said and walked away.

Chapter 7

RAFE TRIED MORE THAN ONCE to read the cake recipe marked with a pink sticky note as Cindy brought her lunch dish into the kitchen. Somehow the words were fuzzy, and he couldn't concentrate.

"I'm going to do some more writing," she said.

He smiled with a nod. "Sounds good."

When she left the room, he put both hands on the counter and hung his head.

Shoot.

He sighed and attempted to read the cake directions again, then shut the cookbook. Not happening. Opening the cupboard, he took out a small glass and poured himself a splash of bourbon. The burn going down his throat averted the regret setting up camp in the middle of his chest.

Now what? Do I just give up or do I go kiss the heck out of her? No. You make the best of the situation. You don't make it harder for her or you.

God, he hated his conscience.

For the hell of it, he picked up his phone to

search for recipes with bourbon in them. Bread pudding with bourbon sauce.

There you go, Rafe. Show her up in the baking department. That will win her heart.

He took another sip of his drink, mentally told his conscience to go take a flying leap, re-read the recipe on his phone, then set to work.

This is the recipe she should have tried. Simple. Although he imagined she might somehow screw up when she got to the bourbon sauce. But he could do that part.

See, that's why you'd be great together. Oh, shut up.

He put the pan into the oven and set the timer to one hour. He walked into the living room and stood in front of Cindy, who sat on the couch typing on her laptop.

"We have an hour," he announced. "How about that haircut?"

"Oh, now?" she said glancing up at him with a surprised expression. "Sure."

She put her laptop aside, got up, and limped a little on her way to the bathroom. She returned with two towels. She lay one of the towels on the floor. "Let's get one of the dining chairs."

Rafe crossed the room and brought the chair back, then sat down. "You can skip the beard," he said. "I'll trim that later."

"Okay," she answered as she opened the black case that held a few different style scissors, setting it on the coffee table next to his chair.

He shook his head at her preparedness.

"What?" she asked, then circled the chair, stood behind him and ran her fingers through his hair, getting a feel for the length, he imagined.

Rafe tipped his head back to look at her. "Is there anything you're not ready for?"

Cindy moved back in front of him, situating herself between his legs and studied him. "Hmm," she murmured. "I wasn't prepared for you."

He put his hands on her hips, tugged her an inch closer as he looked up. "I want to kiss you so much right now, Cyn."

She put her fingers in his hair again, and he closed his eyes at the sensuous tingling of his scalp.

"I know," she said softly. He opened his eyes, searching hers.

"But…" He let go of her hips and rested his hands on his knees.

She tilted her head. "I think kissing would complicate things."

"I guess it would be hard to give me a haircut if you were on my lap and my tongue was in your mouth."

She put her hands on his shoulders and hung her head with a groan.

"At least I know I'm getting to you. Can't blame a man for trying, right?"

She took a step back and he could see a telling flush of desire. She bit her lower lip.

The sexy gesture made him feel he might die. *Not without a fight.*

He tugged his t-shirt off and sat back in the chair, widening his legs to make room for her again.

"Let's do this." Rafe stifled his smirk as she lifted her chin, picked up a comb and scissors, and moved close again.

He put his hands on her behind giving her cheeks a gentle squeeze. "Make it good."

Cindy leaned to set the comb and scissors down next to him on the table. She wrapped her arms around his neck, pulling him into an embrace.

"Rafe," she said with so much longing and heart-melting sadness it broke him.

He slid his hands up her back, his head resting against her breasts as she clung to him.

"I'll stop," he said tenderly and sensed her nod. Giving one more squeeze of his arms he sat back again. "No more teasing."

Even though he backed off, it didn't stop the itch of wanting to touch her as she combed his hair. Eyes closed he focused on the sounds and sensations of her movements. The way the air fluttered whenever she walked around his chair. Her mesmerizing scent when she leaned close. The gentle touch of her fingers as she lifted his hair. The satisfying snip of the scissors.

"Can I touch your beard?" she asked, and he nodded. His eyes lifted to hers as she cupped his face in her hands. "You're so tempting," she whispered.

"Cyn," he warned at the dangerous look of arousal in her eyes. "Are you finished? Because we have to stop."

She stepped back, letting go of his face with a shy smile. "All done."

The immediate sense of loss of her touch overwhelmed him, and he inhaled sharply when the oven timer blared.

"I'll get it," he said his voice rough as he picked up the extra towel and brushed his shoulders before walking to the kitchen. He turned off the timer and paused to gather himself before opening the oven door to set the dish on top of the stove.

Rubbing his hand over his face he returned to the living room as she cleaned up.

"Leave the chair," he said. "I'll put it back after I make the sauce."

"The sauce?" Cindy said, her eyebrows lifting. "Even I know cake doesn't have sauce."

"I made something different. It's a surprise." He walked to the couch to pick up the t-shirt he'd tossed there earlier. "This is the kind of dessert that's best right out of the oven."

She bent to roll the towel on the floor. "Sounds perfect. I didn't really eat my lunch. I'm actually hungry."

"Good. Meet you at the couch when I'm done." He put on his shirt and walked back to the kitchen.

It took about twenty minutes to make the sauce, allowing for it to cool slightly before he added the bourbon. He scooped the dessert into individual dishes, spooned the sauce over the warm pudding, then carried everything to the living room.

Cindy sat with her foot propped up on a pillow and put out her hands when he offered her a bowl. "Whatever this is, it smells amazing."

He smiled. "Bread pudding," he announced. "With bourbon cream sauce."

She dug her spoon in and took a bite. "Oh, that's good."

A moan Rafe absolutely one hundred percent wanted to hear every day for the rest of his life, escaped from somewhere deep inside her.

She's trying to kill me.

He sat down and focused on his own dessert. He glanced her direction, then out the window at the snow-covered mountains and frozen river. The sky was a clear brilliant blue. Snow sparkled like glitter in the air whenever the wind brushed it from the trees. *It's Christmas Eve.* Tomorrow he'd head home. Sometime shortly after Cindy would decide to move to Boston.

"It's so beautiful here," she said.

"It sure is," he agreed. "I can't think of anywhere I'd rather be snowed-in."

"Me too," she said with a drop to her shoulders. "Rafe. I feel like I should say something. I didn't know I'd feel like this."

He grimaced to himself. "Listen, let's keep it simple. Two days ago, I was just the goofy guy who had a huge crush on you and got tongue-tied every time you were near."

She stared at her lap. "You're so much more. You aren't some stranger who got stranded here." She lifted her gaze. "We've known each other for a while. We just didn't…"

"Know we'd get on so well?" he said, finishing her sentence. He put his bowl on the coffee table. When she held out her bowl, he set it aside too.

"I don't want to hurt your feelings," he said.

He caught her small flinch before she turned

away, and he knew she'd already misunderstood him.

"Hey." He took her hand. "I don't know what you're thinking, but you're wrong, okay? I'm in serious..." he pulled back at her startled expression "...something with you. But I'm not interested in only one night. And I don't think I'm cut out for a long-distance relationship."

Rafe could feel tension and it was almost as if he witnessed a shield go up around her.

"I understand. I agree with you. I wouldn't want that either." She smiled, then stood abruptly. "Do you need to pack? What time do you plan to head out tomorrow?"

He lifted his gaze to hers and the pain reflected there crushed his heart.

I didn't mean it.

He glanced out the window. *But you do mean it. That's the problem.*

"Early. Like five," he answered.

She picked up their bowls and walked toward the kitchen, speaking as she left the room. "I'll get up to say Merry Christmas and see you off in the morning."

"I'd like that," he said with as much cheer as he could muster and rubbed his forehead. "I might shut my eyes for a bit right now."

Cindy came back into the room and picked up her laptop from the end table. She patted her belly. "Your bread pudding is amazing. I think I need a nap too."

He clenched his fists to resist pulling her to him, confessing his idiocy and taking every one of his earlier words back.

Her smile didn't reach her eyes before she turned away, walked to the bedroom, and quietly shut the door.

He let his head drop to the back of the couch. *Merry Crappy Christmas.*

Chapter 8

TO HER SURPRISE, CINDY NAPPED for nearly three hours. Her room was almost dark when she awoke in the early evening. She walked to the window and opened the wood blinds, catching the last seconds of the sun before it disappeared behind Mercy Mountain.

In the bathroom, she studied her sullen frown then swiped her index fingers under both eyes to wipe away her smeared mascara. She aggressively rubbed the stupid looking crease on her cheek. The dessert-crashed nap left her crabby and headachy and craving Rafe's bourbon and nasty looking pork rinds for a snack.

What did you expect? You wouldn't drop your life to follow some man around, why should he do that for you?

After she touched up her makeup, she stuck out her tongue at her reflection in the mirror and left the room.

Except for the lights from the Christmas tree and the fire in the fireplace, the living room was dark. Rafe sat on the couch with a beer and the bag of pork rinds on the cushion beside him.

She dropped down next to him. "Give me some of those."

He plopped the bag onto her lap and cracked up. "Looking a little rough there after your nap." His head fell forward laughing.

She tried to maintain a serious expression while stuffing a salty pork rind into her mouth.

"Yeah, whatever," she said chewing and laughing with him.

He got up and walked to the kitchen. "Here," he said, returning. He handed her a glass of water.

"Thanks." She put the bag of chips between them. "These are gross."

He lifted his chin. "If you drink enough, they start to taste better."

"Blech." She took a sip of water and set her glass on the coffee table. "I doubt that."

He glanced at her. "Are we okay?"

She lifted a shoulder. "Of course."

"Do you want to listen to some holiday music?" he asked.

"No." She gave him a wide-eyed incredulous look. "Are you kidding?" She gestured with her hand in the air. "That's your suggestion? Let's sit in the dark, with Christmas lights on and a fire in the fireplace, in a secluded cabin, and then add in romantic music. It's good we both have pork rind breath."

He chuckled. "You ate one pork rind."

She sat back on the couch and picked up the remote. "Let's see if there's a game to watch."

Every now and again as the evening wore on, he got up to add another log to the fire and she to gather better snacks or more beer. Whenever one of them returned to the couch, they settled a little closer. Until finally, his arm rested along the back of the couch, and she was tucked against his shoulder, her hand resting on the middle of his chest.

When the game ended, she sat up and rubbed her cheeks. "You better get some sleep. You have a long drive tomorrow."

Rafe nodded as they picked up the snacks and empty bottles to carry everything to the kitchen.

"Leave it." She walked by him with a friendly pat to his arm then headed toward her bedroom. *Don't look back.* "I'll clean things up tomorrow. I'll set my alarm and see you in the morning."

"Good night, Cindy."

"Good night," she said and shut her door.

In the early morning, still in bed, Cindy listened as Rafe left the cabin and she heard him start his truck to warm up. She picked up her phone to check the time and dismissed her alarm set to go off five minutes later. Sitting on the edge of the bed, she clasped her hands holding them under her chin.

Chin up, Cindy. It's Christmas.

She smiled at an image she conjured of Rafe's parents happy for his arrival, even though she had no idea what that would look like. In a couple hours, she'd call her mother and her older brothers to speak with her nieces and nephews one-by-one.

She put on her robe, freshened up in the bathroom then headed out to the kitchen to make coffee.

"Merry Christmas," she said a few minutes later when Rafe entered the cabin and stomped snow from his boots on the mat.

"Merry Christmas," he said with a bright smile.

"I made some coffee for the road." She walked to the door and handed him a thermos.

"I appreciate it. Thanks."

She put her hands in her robe pockets and took a step back.

"Well, have a safe trip. Please tell your parents Merry Christmas and that I'm sorry about all this."

She bit the inside of her cheek, finding the pain an antidote to her heart's traitorous drop to the floor.

He lowered his chin. "Cyn."

"Goodbye," she added with a ridiculous wave.

"Do you think I'm leaving here without a hug?" He opened his arms.

She went full in, her arms wrapped around him, her head resting on his chest as he rubbed her back and tucked his face into her neck. He kissed her cheek, put on his hat, and opened the door.

"Text me when you get there, okay?" she asked.

He shook his head. "I don't text. I'll call. After eleven hours, I'll want to hear your voice."

She put her hands to her chest. "Me too." She

sniffled aware that her eyes brimmed with tears. "Okay, go on." She waved her hand shooing him along.

Rafe chuckled. "Bye."

Cindy smiled with a nod before closing the door. After a long pause, his boots thumped on the steps then crunched on the snow-covered path.

She turned, faced the empty cabin, and tightened the ties of her robe. No use going back to bed. She walked to the kitchen and poured herself a mug of coffee and sat alone at the table-for-two.

Rafe had just driven out of the parking area at the cabins and reached the bottom of the hill before the main road when his phone buzzed.

Don't let me have forgotten something. I cannot go back.

"Merry Christmas, Dude!" His buddy Jim bellowed into his ear when he answered.

"Merry Christmas," he said with a chuckle. "Why are you up so early?"

"Sofia and I have lodge duties with the guests before the family heads to the ranch for our own Christmas," Jim answered.

"Hi Rafe!" he could hear Jim's wife, Sofia, in the background. "Put him on speaker. Hi Rafe," she repeated. "Merry Christmas. How are your mom and dad?"

"Not sure yet. I'm still in Colorado."

"What happened?" Jim asked.

He took a deep breath, grateful they couldn't see his expression. "I was helping Doc Cindy get to the cabin she's staying at in Hawkeye and with the storm I got snowed in there."

A muffled crash sounded like the phone dropped on the other end.

"Rafe," Sofia said his name in a low voice he'd never heard from her before. "You've been stuck in a cabin alone with Doc Cindy all this time?" She giggled. "Oh my God."

He laughed at the sound of her clapping. "Uh, huh."

"Dude." Jim's voice came on again. "Where are you now?"

"I just left. I'm about to turn onto the main road through the canyon."

"Did you kiss her?" Sofia asked.

"No."

"What the hell?" Jim asked. "Why not?"

"Yeah, what the hell, Dude?" Sofia repeated. "Can you believe this? I'm the one that introduced him to Cindy because he has such a huge crush on her, and he doesn't even kiss her when he gets the chance?"

"I know, right?" Jim responded.

Rafe cleared his throat. "Hello. I'm still here too."

"Did you get all tongue-tied and fuss it up or something? Did you make a move? Oh no, did she push you away?" Sofia asked.

"No. Geez. You have no faith in me, do you?"

"Tell us what happened." Jim said.

Rafe sighed. "She has a job offer from Boston.

She's probably going to take it." He paused. "It's one thing to have a crush on her. It'd be another thing to get a taste of what could be and then have her leave. I couldn't do it. Plus, she needs to make her decision…it's better this way."

"Shoot," Jim said. "I'm sorry, buddy."

"Yeah. It's okay," he said.

He listened to more scuffling noises and then Sofia's voice came on again. "Rafe, you need to go back to the cabin and kiss her. Pronto."

He scoffed. "That's not happening. One, I just left and two, I explained why that isn't a good idea. This is not a corny movie." He regretted his last remark the minute it left his mouth. Sofia was not a woman who gave up easily. Plus, she really had been the person most nurturing his growing friendship with Cindy.

"I want you to turn your truck around," Sofia said in a misleadingly calm voice, "right now, go back to the cabin and kiss Cindy."

"You can't tell me what to do, bossy girl," he said just to get her goat.

"That was a mistake," Jim shouted in the background.

"Listen to me closely, Mooney," Sofia continued.

His laugh boomed whenever she referred to him by his last name.

"I said listen to me. You just left Cindy all alone. To make a major life decision."

"Yes," Rafe said.

"With only one offer on the table."

"What are you saying?"

She sighed exasperated. "Cindy has one thing to consider. The job in Boston. Yes or no. Go give her something else to think about. Something to weigh that decision against."

He sat back in his seat. "You really think I can kiss that well, honey?"

"Mooney, you are a big strapping, former military hottie. You're damn right I think you can kiss that well. Now turn that truck around, mister and get up after that woman. Show her what you're made of."

He laughed so hard he almost missed out on Jim's admonishment of his wife.

"Hottie? Seriously, Sofia? Hand me the phone," Jim said. "Rafe, good God man, just do what Sofia says or neither one of us will ever hear the end of it. Call me later and let us know what happens. Merry Christmas. Go get her, tiger."

The call abruptly ended. Rafe stared at his phone. He twisted his neck trying to release the sudden stiffness, then put the truck in reverse, turned around, drove back up the hill and parked.

This is either the best idea or the worst idea ever. He got out of the vehicle and marched toward the cabin. When his boots thumped on the steps, there was no going back. Unless Cindy happened to be in the shower, she'd have heard him coming by now.

He froze when the front door swung open. He stared at her adorableness, in her robe and slippers, her hair ruffled from sleep.

"Rafe? Did you forget something?"

"Did I." He cringed. "I mean, yes, I did."

Cindy pressed her lips together. "Tell me what it is. I'll go get it for you."

"Right here, it is." Rafe whipped off his hat. "Damn it, I'm all befuddled again."

She stepped onto the porch, letting the door shut behind her. "Why did you come back?"

He put his hat on the wood bench next to the front door and removed his gloves setting them down also. Unzipping his coat, he then moved in front of her, fixing his eyes on hers. With one hand behind her neck and another on her lower back he tugged her against him and lowered his head.

"Cyn," he growled, his lips hovering so close he could feel her warm sigh. "I've never wanted to kiss anyone the way I want to kiss you." He barely brushed his lips to hers and lifted his head. "You make me a stuttering fool. But I don't care just as long as I get to be near you."

She pressed against him and put her hands on his chest.

"I know you may leave –"

"Shut up," Cindy whispered with a gleam in her eye. "Are you going to kiss me, or not?"

Rafe tightened his hold. "Oh, yeah. I'm going to kiss you and you're going to think about it, just like I am, every minute of every hour until I come back. And if that's unfair –"

She let her forehead fall against his chest. "You're still talking."

"Look at me, honey."

She lifted her head, and he pressed his lips to hers then sucked her tongue into his mouth swallowing her gasp. This was not a kiss that allowed coming up for air. The press of his hips left no doubt how hot he was for her. A low moan escaped deep inside as he savaged her mouth.

He broke the kiss, grumbling, "hold on," as he opened the door behind her and walked her backward inside the cabin. Out of the cold, Rafe untied her robe and grabbed her bottom in both hands. Heat scorched his heart at the exquisite softness of her breasts smashed against his chest. He crushed his lips to hers again. When he finally pulled away, she stared up at him. He gloated inside when she ran a finger around her lips.

"My knees are wobbling," she said.

"Merry Christmas." He leaned in to place a kiss on her forehead. "I'll call you tonight."

Rafe opened the cabin door, grabbed his gloves from the bench, put on his hat, then walked back to his truck with a satisfied grin. Steps seven, eight, nine. Mouth to mouth. Hands to cute little butt. Something about torsos.

Who cares? Every thrilling touch was worth it.

Chapter 9

IT WAS LATE MORNING BEFORE Cindy managed to change out of her pajamas into a pair of yoga pants and the fluffy forest green sweater her mother had sent as a gift. She'd done the requisite facetime opening gifts virtually with her family. Most of it while in a stupor, often staring at the Christmas tree as she reveled in every tantalizing memory of Rafe's kiss.

At noon, she ate another helping of bread pudding, drank two fingers of bourbon, then fell asleep on the couch for thirty minutes.

I'm going to bake that cake with frosting she decided when she woke. It would be several hours until Rafe would call her.

"I don't text," he'd announced and even recalling *that* turned her on. She did like the idea he wouldn't be distracted on the road.

That's just basic safety.

She held up the new apron from her oldest brother. *I'm so good, Santa came twice.*

She shook her head and threw it on top of the

other aprons, then riffled through the pile and pulled out the red polka-dot style. She poured herself another small drink then spread the apron flat on the coffee table.

Put it on. Why not?

She walked to the front door to lock it, then closed all the wood blinds in the cabin and shut the curtains over the kitchen sink in the kitchen. At the thermostat, Cindy turned up the heat to seventy-five degrees.

In her bedroom, she left her yoga pants on, but removed the green sweater and her bra then pulled the red apron over her head. The front barely covered her nipples when she examined herself in the bathroom mirror turning side-to-side. She shrugged and tied the strings tight behind her back. She returned to the living room, stopping at the turntable to put on a Christmas album and cranked up the volume.

"I'm not even going to write down the recipe," she said out loud on her way back to the kitchen. She pulled a beer from the refrigerator.

Fifteen minutes later she stuck the two round cake pans in the oven and closed the door. She glanced down at her apron covered with batter.

"On to the frosting," she announced before heading to the living room to choose a new holiday album.

"I feel good," she added with a nod to the tree. She picked up the bottle of bourbon from the coffee table, stopping to take a swig.

Back in the kitchen, she leaned her elbows on the counter as she sipped a second beer while reading over the frosting recipe. That seems simple enough. She studied the instructions for constructing a piping cone out of parchment paper to decorate the cake with.

Like that will happen.

When the record on the stereo skipped, she walked off-kilter to the turntable to move the needle to the next song.

"I may be tipsy, but I'm determined," she shouted before she shushed herself.

That's me. Always determined. About what exactly?

The oven timer buzzed, startling her from her dazed state. Donning potholder mitts, she opened the oven door and lifted each cake pan out to the stovetop.

Picking up her beer from the counter, she took a gulp and stared at the cake. It dawned on her she didn't give two shits about decorating them, nor her incessant need to make the most difficult desserts every year. She turned to squint at her stupid flip chart mocking her from the corner of the kitchen.

Cindy slapped a mitt-covered hand to her cheek.

"What's the point if the outcome isn't something you want." She flung her arms wide and spun. "I get it."

Whoa. No spinning.

Cindy clung to the counter and glanced at the clock on the wall. Taking off her oven mitts she counted from five in the morning forward on her fingers. Eleven hours. That's four o'clock if Rafe doesn't make any stops. Maybe four-thirty if he makes a stop. Of course, he'd make a stop. She paused.

What's my point here? Pretty sure you're drunk.

"Right," she answered out loud. Cindy grabbed a glass from the cupboard and walked to the sink. "Water." She filled her glass, drank it, and refilled.

She left the kitchen and flopped down on the couch. Picking up her phone she took what she thought was a sexy selfie in her apron and drank her second glass of water.

He's going to call me.

The thought half-sobered her and she stood, walking purposely toward the bathroom as she pulled the apron over her head, allowing it drop to the floor behind her. Turning on the shower, she let the water warm as she removed the rest of her clothes then stepped under the spray.

Five minutes later she turned off the water, wrapped her head in a towel, put on her robe and lay on the bed.

It was many hours later when her phone rang, and she sat straight up. She hobbled to the living room, nearly crumbling to the floor when she stubbed her big toe on the edge of the coffee table.

"Hi," she answered out of breath.

"Hi." Rafe chuckled. "Did you run to the phone?"

Cindy tugged the lapel of her robe closed. "Sort of. I fell asleep. What time is it?"

"Five-thirty."

She glanced at darkness outside the front window. "It's later than I thought. Was the drive, okay?"

"It was fine. I forgot the whipped cream. I had to make a stop before I got to the house."

"Oh, shoot." She laughed. "I'm sorry. We wrote a note and everything."

"I take it as a good sign. I assume you had other things to think about today." He paused. "Am I right?"

She grinned at her delighted face reflected in the window. "Yes. I thought about our kiss."

"Good," he answered.

"Did you?"

"Are you kidding me?" Rafe's deep voice rumbled. "I nearly drove off the road a few times. So, what else did you do all day?"

Cindy moved to the couch. She told him about the fluffy sweater from her mother and the newest obscene apron from her brothers.

"And I got a little drunk, so I made a cake but didn't frost it. I wore the red apron."

"You wore the red apron without me?"

She snickered. "You sound so sad."

"I'm heartbroken. That's for special occasions."

"Hold on." She held her phone in front of her and pulled up her photos. When she found the selfie she took earlier, she started laughing. It was her all right. But only her chest in the apron plus the bottom of her chin.

"What's so funny?" Rafe asked.

"I took a selfie in the apron, but I was a little tipsy so it's not very good."

"Send it anyway."

"No." She giggled.

"It's Christmas. Send the photo. Wait, hold on, Cyn."

She listened as Rafe spoke to one of his parents. "It's a photo just for me, Mom."

"Rafe, don't tell her that," she whispered into the phone. "It sounds like I'm sending a naked picture."

His laugh boomed. "Hold on, she wants to say hello."

"Dr. Wheeler? This is Maria Mooney, Rafe's mother."

Cindy pulled her lapel closed again, patting her still damp hair as if her disheveled state could be seen.

"Mrs. Mooney. Merry Christmas. Please, you can call me Cindy. I'm sure you're so happy to finally have Rafe arrive. I'm truly sorry for causing his delay."

"Aw, Rafe," his mother said. "I like her. She's so polite."

She heard him chuckle followed by, "She can hear you, Mom."

"Cindy?"

"Yes, Mrs. Mooney?"

"Tom, that's Rafe's father, and I want you to visit us next time Rafe comes to town. Okay, sweetheart? Rafe says you have trouble with the baking. I can help."

Cindy covered her mouth with her hand to keep from laughing and sat back on the couch.

"I'm sorry about that," Rafe said, coming back on the line. "She has no filter."

Cindy laughed. "She's adorable. Tell her I like

her too."

"I will. Hey, we're going to eat now so I have to go."

She smiled. "Okay, enjoy dinner."

Rafe sighed. "I know it's too soon to ask if you've made up your mind yet, but when you make a final decision about Boston, will you call me?"

"Yes." She pulled her legs up on the couch, tucking her robe over them. "You'll be first to know. I promise."

"Text me the photo."

"I thought you didn't text."

"I'll make an exception. Merry Christmas, Cyn."

"Good night, Rafe."

She put her phone on the coffee table and rubbed her stubbed toe. Then picked up the apron from the floor where she dropped it earlier. She considered the idea of taking a new photograph, then sat on the couch and scrolled to the apron picture again.

That's a lot of side-boobs.

She put a hand over her racing heart, selected the photo to share, typed *Merry Christmas*, hit send, and closed her eyes. She lifted her phone when it vibrated ten seconds later to read his reply.

Cyn…you're beautiful.

Chapter 10

Two days after Christmas, Cindy woke early, sat up in bed, and spent the next three hours finishing the edits to her book. She attached the final manuscript to an email and added a short note to her publisher, once again reiterating, "No ladders on the cover," and hit send.

After showering and getting dressed, she spent the next forty-five minutes cleaning up the kitchen, including tossing the cakes she'd left on the stove, pans, and all, into the garbage. She loaded all her pie plates, baking utensils, and cookbooks into a blue plastic tub with wheels and a handle. She poured the remaining bourbon down the drain and rinsed the bottle, breathing through her mouth to avoid the smell of liquor.

Carrying the flip chart from the room, she grabbed a red marker and made a list of people to email. It was the Tuesday after Christmas. She wouldn't be able to do more than leave voicemails or emails.

When she finished, she powered down her laptop and put it back in her bag. With one final checkmark, she ripped the page off her chart, crumpled it, lit a match, and tossed the flaming list into the fireplace.

She sat at the dining table-for-two and put on her boots, then put on her coat, hat, and gloves. She pulled the blue tub full of baking supplies out onto the porch. The day was gorgeous. Crisp, bright, and bitterly cold. She inhaled the fresh winter air and walked down the two steps letting the tub clatter and bounce behind her. Marching down the hill she was careful not to slip on any ice.

Mr. Clack opened the door of his office a second after she knocked.

"Good morning, Cindy. Did you decide to check out early?"

"No. Actually, I was hoping I could stay through New Year's. Would that be a problem?"

He shook his head. "Not at all."

"Great, thank you. Does your wife bake?"

"Does my wife bake? Uh, sure, Sylvia bakes. Why do you ask?"

"I don't bake," Cindy announced and opened the top of the tub. "These are baking supplies. Do you think she'd be interested in having them?"

Mr. Clack took a step toward the tub with a glance down. "You don't want all this?"

"Nope. I was just going to throw it away but figured I'd see if you thought Sylvia would like to have any of it first."

"Thank you. I'm sure she'd make use of all of

it."

"Good," she said with a beaming smile as she closed the lid and offered him the handle. "Happy New Year to both of you."

"Happy New Year." Mr. Clack chuckled. "Give me a ring if you need anything at the cabin."

Cindy thanked him and left the office, taking a short walk along the path between the other cabins on her way back to her own. She stood on the snow-covered back deck, looking at the trees, Mercy Mountain, and the frozen Talking Fish River below.

No more hiding behind achievements Cindy. This is home.

She considered the counseling business she wanted to start. Her very own practice with appointments in the towns of Ashnee Valley and Four Bears. Somehow Nicki, the athletic girl, and her family Rafe mentioned, also came to mind. *Maybe I can help there too.*

Her heart fluttered when she thought about Rafe. His handsome face. That sexy beard. The way he accepted her need for perfection. His deep, growly voice when he said her name.

Cyn.

She wrapped her arms around herself and lifted her face to the sun.

How many years have I misinterpreted hope as nervousness and shied away from the intensity of my passions?

When she counseled others, this repression was a way of being she spotted easily. Now, gently, gradually, she allowed entry to her self-awareness.

She walked around the cabin and went inside. She sat on the couch enjoying the Christmas tree lights.

There is nothing more you need to do, be, say, prove, or achieve.

The sentiment landed softly, so she repeated the words to herself like a vow. As the sun went down over the mountain, she reached for her phone. One more call to make.

"Hey," Rafe answered. "I was hoping I'd hear from you. How was your day?"

"I made the decision." Cindy waited for a response. "Rafe?"

"I'm here. Hold on. Let me go upstairs."

She suffered through the torturous seconds of silence before Rafe came back on the line. "Okay, I'm ready."

It wasn't in her nature to be coy in this moment. "I'm staying."

She heard the whoosh of his exhale and kept talking. "I declined the job in Boston. I finished my book. I'm starting my own practice in Ashnee Valley and Four Bears." She took a deep breath. "I've quit baking."

"That last one was hardest to say, wasn't it?"

"I'm a quitter..." she announced with confidence "... and I'm proud of it."

He cracked up. She pressed her lips together listening to his laughter.

"When are you coming back?" she asked.

"Cyn, you know damn well I'm going to drive all night to get to you."

Her circuits went haywire making all her lady

bits pulse. She sucked in air.

"I'm hoping you're the one tongue-tied right now," Rafe continued. "The silence is killing me."

"Yes. Drive now. And Rafe?"

"Yeah, honey?"

"I'm in deep fluster with you."

"Cyn." Rafe groaned her name. "I'm in deep too, sweetheart. I'll see you soon."

The call ended and she hugged her cell phone to her chest and glanced around the cabin. She visualized a version of herself going all sexy vixen on Rafe when he arrived. She'd open the door wearing only the red apron and holding a beautiful steaming pie fresh out of the oven.

That's not you.

Cindy forced herself to remain sitting for several minutes, then stood, confident in her alternate plan. She picked up her purse and keys heading out the door to the small grocery store in town.

Late morning the next day she heard the crunch of tires on snow. Peeking out the kitchen window she watched Rafe park his truck in front of the cabin. She turned the oven on warm and stuck the foil-covered tray inside. She grabbed two beers from the fridge then kicked the door shut with her foot. She glanced at the living room.

Game on TV. Christmas tree lights on. Fire in the fireplace. She set the beers on the table-for-two and walked to the front door.

Before he could knock, she flung the door

wide and struck as provocative a pose as possible while leaning against the doorframe in her footy pajamas.

Rafe dropped his duffel bag next to his feet. "You look exactly how I hoped."

"You do too." She stepped to the side, gesturing for him to come in. "I made nachos," she said proudly while he removed his coat and hung it on the hook by the door. "There's beer and a game on TV."

He sat on the chair by the door and took off his boots, a boyish sort of smile growing the more she spoke.

"Come here," he said and offered his hand to gently pull her onto his lap and bury his nose in her neck.

"There's no dessert," she murmured as he hugged her close and kissed the delicate skin behind her ear.

"Help me warm up first," he said in a dark masculine voice as he unbuttoned the front of her pajamas and slipped his hands inside.

She shivered with pleasure at the cold shock of his fingers touching her breasts.

He sat back, staring into her eyes with sudden intensity as he caressed her lovingly. "Can we eat later?"

She shifted on his lap, her hand to his cheek, and nodded.

"You know this is more than just flustered. I drove all night to get to you. I want to make love to you, Cyn."

Her heart pounded as she wrapped her arms

around his neck, holding on when he stood with her in his arms and carried her to the bedroom.

"We only have a few more days to step eleven with each other until it's the new year."

Cindy laughed at his serious tone. "Since I'm staying, we could practice all the steps next year too."

Rafe lay her on the bed, his eyes raking over her. "Good point."

"You make me happy," Cindy said, touching her fingers to his beard.

He gazed at her with tender amusement. "Cyn, I'm in love with you. I feel like the luckiest man alive to be here with you right now."

She pulled Rafe in for a kiss, sighing when his weight settled over her body, and she embraced all her hopes and love for the new year.

Acknowlegements

Thank you, Laurie Cooper, and Pub-Craft. Can you believe this is publication of four books already? And now we're heading to nearby Four Bears on the other side of Mercy Mountain for more stories. Thank you for all you do to promote this series and for making it fun.

Thank you to my editor Barbara Bettis who knows all the Ashnee Valley characters so well and helps them shine. I love the wonderful holiday cover for *Cozy Christmas Crush* that Kim Killion designed. Thank you, Jennifer Jakes for making sure everything happens on time and smoothly.

To my husband and son, your positive encouragement and love are the best gifts.

To readers and especially those who write reviews, you are treasured by all authors. Thank you.

Happy Holidays!

Books by Becca Maxton

MERCY MOUNTAIN SERIES

Dragonfly Dance
Firefly Duet
Honeybee Rhythm
Cozy Christmas Crush

For sneak peeks and the latest release dates
visit *www.beccamaxton.com*

About the Author

Becca Maxton is a contemporary romance author. She writes sensuous (dare say, steamy) and encouraging stories about rocky road detours leading to resilience and romance. Her characters are brave women and men facing challenges together and finding love.

Becca lives in Colorado with her husband and son. Follow Becca Maxton on Facebook and Instagram *@BeccaMaxtonAuthor* or visit *www.beccamaxton.com*. She enjoys meeting and connecting with readers online.

Manufactured by Amazon.ca
Bolton, ON